Wilczek's for as he tapped out the series of commands that would give him control over the computer system he had designed.

Suddenly he froze. Flashing onto the monitor was the image of a man standing in the stainless steel elevator.

"Going down," the computer announced.

The man's mouth opened wide. He lost his footing as the floor dropped out from under him.

He was thrown against the wall, his head smashing against the stainless steel as the elevator plummeted.

"No!" Wilczek screamed.

His scream died in his throat as the scene on the screen jumped, then flickered like a candle.

The last thing he saw was the man's legs twitching, then becoming motionless as the picture went black.

"Program executed," the computer said.

Other X-Files books

#1 X Marks the Spot
#2 Darkness Falls
#3 Tiger, Tiger
#4 Squeeze
#5 Humbug
#6 Shapes
#7 Fear
#8 Voltage
#9 E. B. E.
#10 Die, Bug, Die!
#11 Ghost in the Machine

Voyager

THE X FILES

GHOST IN THE MACHINE

A novel by Les Martin

Based on the television series
The X-Files created by
Chris Carter

Based on the teleplay
written by Howard Gordon
and Alex Gansa

HarperCollins*Publishers*

To all you wonderful dark people out there

Voyager
An Imprint of HarperCollins*Publishers*
77–85 Fulham Palace Road,
Hammersmith, London W6 8JB

First paperback edition 1997
1 2 3 4 5 6 7 8 9

First published in the USA by HarperTrophy
A division of HarperCollins*Publishers* 1997

The X-Files™ © Twentieth Century Fox Film Corporation 1997
All rights reserved

Cover photograph © Twentieth Century Fox Corporation 1997
Cover photo by Michael Levine

ISBN 0 00 648313 5

Set in Century

Printed and bound in Great Britain by
Caledonian International Book Manufacturing Ltd, Glasgow

All rights reserved. No part of this publication may be
reproduced, stored in a retrieval system, or transmitted,
in any form or by any means, electronic, mechanical,
photocopying, recording or otherwise, without the prior
permission of the publishers.

This book is sold subject to the condition that it shall not,
by way of trade or otherwise, be lent, re-sold, hired out or
otherwise circulated without the publisher's prior consent
in any form of binding or cover other than that in which it
is published and without a similar condition including this
condition being imposed on the subsequent purchaser.

GHOST IN THE MACHINE

Chapter ONE

Crystal City, Virginia. Home of the Eurisko Building, the world headquarters of the Eurisko Corporation. Sheathed in dark glass, the skyscraper jutted thirty stories into the air. You could almost hear it say, "I am your future."

Right now, in a huge office on the top floor of the building, two men argued about that future.

You only had to look at them to realize how differently they saw things.

One of them wore an expensive suit that fit him to perfection. His full head of graying hair was neatly shaped. He stood behind a very large and very neatly organized desk.

The man across from him wore a dark T-shirt and faded jeans that hung loosely on his wire-thin body. Uncombed dark hair bushed out around his head. But what you saw first was the intense gleam in his eyes behind the metal-rimmed glasses.

The thin man was Brad Wilczek, founder of the Eurisko Corporation.

"Why do you think Eurisko's stock price has dropped like a lead weight?" he demanded.

THE X-FILES

The other man, Eurisko CEO Benjamin Drake, smiled. It was the smile of a man talking to a child who was having a temper tantrum.

"Profits were poor last year," Drake said. "And they won't improve this year unless we reduce costs."

"Wrong," Wilczek snapped. "It's because you've cut the budget for research and development in half. You're forgotten that the business of Eurisko is tomorrow, not today. You've forgotten what the adventure is all about."

The smile stayed on Drake's face. "Like it or not, the computer software business is changing," he said. "We're not an infant industry anymore. We're playing hardball against the big boys. We have to be lean and mean. We have to cut the fat."

"What we have to cut is fat cat greed," Wilczek said. "We have to sacrifice short-term profits for long-term goals."

"Let's not go through this again," said Drake. "We already had this debate at our stockholders' meeting. And you know which side they voted for. Who are you trying to impress? The scanner up there?"

Drake glanced at the ceiling. A red light glowed on an electronic eye connected to the building's Central Operating System or COS. With hundreds of other scanners all over the building, the system kept tabs on everything going on from the basement to the top floor.

Wilczek glared at Drake. "Don't you get it? You're killing me. You're killing my company."

Drake's smile stayed in place. "Eurisko isn't your company, Brad," he reminded Wilczek. "Not anymore. Better grow up and get used to it. Now, why don't you go and let me do my job."

Drake watched Wilczek storm out. Then he took off his jacket and sat down at his laptop to write the announcement of the change in command at Eurisko.

It was night when Drake finished. He reread his final paragraph: "As my first major act, I am ending the COS project. Despite our high hopes, its dismal sales and rising costs make no other choice possible."

Drake nodded with satisfaction, pressed the Save key, then shut down his laptop. Yawning, he stood up and stretched, put on his jacket, and headed for the door.

Before he reached it, he heard the sound of running water. It came from the bathroom of the executive office.

Grimacing, Drake went to see what the trouble was.

His feet sloshed in water on the tile bathroom floor. The light coming in through the open door

THE X-FILES

let him see water overflowing from the black marble sink. He went to look more closely. The faucet was on, and the drain seemed stopped up.

"Another reason to terminate COS," he muttered. "If it can't even run this building right."

He went to the sink and passed his hand over the faucet. The water flow stopped. *At least this electronic control works,* he thought.

The basin, though, stayed full. Drake took off his jacket, rolled up his sleeve, and plunged his hand into the water to try to free up the drain.

Before he could finish the job the phone in the bathroom rang.

"If it's not one thing, it's another," sighed Drake, and yanked his hand out of the water. After shaking it to get rid of some of the moisture, he picked up the phone.

"Hello," he said curtly.

There was silence.

"Hello," he repeated, more sharply.

A computer-generated voice came over the line. "At the tone, Eastern Standard Time will be seven thirty-five P.M.—"

The sound of the door slamming drowned out the rest of the message. The bathroom was plunged into darkness. Drake heard the electronic lock on the door snap into place.

GHOST IN THE MACHINE

"What the—?" he said.

He hung up the phone. He went to the door and felt for the magnetic card key slot. He slid his card through the slot, then tried the door handle. No luck.

"Rats," said Drake. "I guess I'll have to try the old-fashioned way."

He took a key ring from his pocket. He felt for the heavy key he needed and found the keyhole. He inserted the key and—

A fireball exploded in the bathroom.

The flash was the last thing Drake ever saw.

His body flew backward through darkness and slammed into the bathroom mirror.

Benjamin Drake landed on his back on the wet tile floor, hands and arms outstretched, his body motionless. Above him, the red light of the scanner glowed ominously.

Chapter TWO

Halloween was coming, and a plastic jack-o'-lantern decorated the bull pen at FBI Headquarters. Special Agent Jerry Lamana stared at it. The jack-o'-lantern grinned back. Of the two, the jack-o'-lantern looked a little more intelligent.

To be fair to Jerry, he was not really stupid. He just was not very smart.

He had done one smart thing at the FBI, though. He had been Special Agent Fox Mulder's partner for a year. Jerry looked back on that year fondly. It had been fun to actually solve cases. Which was why he had come into the bull pen looking for Mulder now.

At the moment, though, he couldn't stop looking at the candy balls that filled the jack-o'-lantern.

He knew he shouldn't have any. He was fifteen pounds overweight, according to his last FBI physical.

Still, one candy ball wouldn't hurt. Besides, he needed the energy.

His hand snaked into the jack-o'-lantern. It came out stuffed with candy balls. He popped one

GHOST IN THE MACHINE

into his mouth and dropped the others into his jacket pocket. You never knew when you would need a quick pick-me-up. This job was one emergency after another. Sometimes Jerry wished he hadn't watched so many cops-and-robbers shows when he was a kid. Then he might have gone into some other line of work. But he had invested too much time in the FBI to write it off now.

Jerry scanned the room. His gaze darted among the agents shooting the breeze, sipping coffee, and grabbing lunch. His face lit up when he spotted Mulder.

Mulder and his partner, Special Agent Dana Scully, were getting lunch at a food cart.

They turned around when a voice boomed, "Mulder!"

Mulder forced a smile when he saw who it was. "Hey, Jerry," he said. "Good to see you."

Jerry gave him an eager smile in return. Mulder found it easy to imagine Jerry as a puppy dog, madly wagging his tail.

Then Jerry shifted his smile toward Scully and stuck out his hand.

"Dana Scully, right?" Jerry said as they shook hands. "I'm Jerry Lamana. Mulder probably told you about me."

"Nice to meet you," Scully said. She raised her

THE X-FILES

eyebrows toward Mulder in a silent question.

"Jerry and I worked together in Violent Crimes," Mulder explained.

"Hey, what's this 'worked together' stuff?" asked Jerry heartily. "We did more than just 'work together.' We were real partners, right, partner?"

"Yeah, right, of course," Mulder said, looking at his salad with great interest.

Meanwhile, Scully had chosen a tuna sandwich on seven-grain bread. The man running the food cart glanced at the tray Mulder and Scully shared. "That comes to eight-fifty," he said.

"My turn, Mulder," said Scully, opening her purse.

Jerry whipped out his wallet. "I'm buying you two lunch," he announced, pulling out a ten. He slapped it on the food cart as if it were a hundred.

"Why, uh, thanks," Scully said, and gave Mulder another puzzled look.

Mulder, though, wasn't puzzled.

"Having trouble on a case, Jerry?" he asked mildly.

"Matter of fact—" Jerry began. Then he paused and looked around. "Look, maybe we could discuss this in private."

"We can go to my office," Mulder said, spearing a cherry tomato.

GHOST IN THE MACHINE

"Good idea," Jerry said. He turned to Scully. "Of course, you're welcome to come along. Three heads are better than two."

"Be glad to," Scully said, curious now.

"I can even offer you dessert," said Jerry, pulling out a couple of candy balls.

When the three of them entered Mulder's basement office, Jerry shook his head. "Never could figure why the brass stuck you down here," he said. "A bright guy like you."

Then Jerry looked around Mulder's office and shook his head again. "Never understood how you could work in all this clutter. Me, I like things nice and neat."

"Some of the cases I deal with are . . . messy," Mulder said, waiting for Jerry to get to the point.

He didn't have to wait long.

"Matter of fact, the case I'm on now is kind of messy," Jerry said. "You probably heard about it. The CEO of the Eurisko Corporation was found fried in his private office. The cause of death was electrocution."

"It wasn't accidental?" Scully asked.

"Doesn't look that way," Jerry said. "Looks like some kind of elaborate booby trap. But we don't know how it worked or who set it up. The building engineer found the corpse just twelve hours ago."

THE X-FILES

"Why is the FBI on the case?" Mulder asked.

"Eurisko has some government contracts," Jerry said. "National security could be involved."

"Are we talking about weaponry?" asked Mulder.

"Not according to our info," said Jerry. "Of course, you never know. But it could be other government programs. You use computer software for all kinds of stuff."

"Who's running the investigation?" Scully wanted to know.

"You know Nancy Spiller?" Jerry responded.

"The forensics instructor at the FBI Academy?" asked Scully. "Our official guru on death and its causes?"

"Yeah, her," Jerry said.

"I remember taking her course," said Scully. "We used to call her the Iron Maiden."

"That's on her good days," said Jerry. "One mistake, and the spikes go into you. Anyway, she's putting together the team on this and . . ."

Jerry paused, cleared his throat, and turned to Mulder. "After she picked me, I took the liberty of suggesting your name."

Mulder stiffened. "Look, Jerry, I'd like to help you out on this," he said. "But we're not on general assignment. Agent Scully and I have been channeled into special investigations."

GHOST IN THE MACHINE

"Yeah, I know," Jerry said. "The X-files. That's where you went when we split up as a team. I remember, you didn't really think it was my kind of thing."

"As you said, we're different types," commented Mulder. "Neat and messy. You were better suited for Violent Crimes. They're usually on the . . . simple side. You know, nice and neat."

"Not this one," Jerry said. "Look, Mulder, I don't like to beg—but I need your help. I don't want to drop the ball on this one."

"You won't drop the ball, Jerry," Mulder said. He hoped he sounded more convinced than he was.

Jerry sighed. "This case is too heavy for me to take the chance. The dead man, Benjamin Drake, wasn't just CEO of a giant corporation. He was a close friend of the Attorney General. It would be a real feather in my cap to nail the killer. Believe me, I could use one."

Mulder began again. "Jerry, I'd like to help you, but . . ."

"Come on, Mulder," said Jerry. "Have a heart. For old times' sake."

Scully smiled to herself as she saw Mulder hesitate.

She knew Mulder could not pass a panhandler without forking over some coins, or go by a fallen bird without trying to get it back into its nest.

"Well, no promises," said Mulder. "But I'll see what I can do."

He glanced at Scully.

"What *we* can do," she said.

Chapter THREE

The next morning Mulder and Scully stood in the plaza in front of the Eurisko Building and looked up and up at it. Sunlight blazed off its mirrorlike surface. Reflected in the glass were blue sky and drifting white clouds.

"Wow," said Scully, blinking. "This is your kind of place, Mulder. It looks like it dropped down here from outer space."

"It came from cyberspace," Mulder said. "The house that software built. And from what I've read, software runs it, as well. There was an article about it in a computer magazine. The title was 'High tech goes sky-high.' It seems a giant computer operates the entire building."

"Looks like a nice place to visit, but . . ." said Scully, and shook her head.

"Well, let's see it from the inside," Mulder said. "Time to give Jerry a helping hand."

"Level with me, Mulder," Scully said as they walked toward the entrance. "Why did you and Jerry split up?"

"Because I'm a pain to work with," Mulder said.

"Seriously, Mulder," Scully said.

13

"I'm not a pain?" asked Mulder.

"Mulder, come on," Scully said.

Before Mulder could answer, they both had to show their IDs to the guard at the entrance.

As they went through the door, Mulder continued, "Let's say Jerry and I had different career goals. Jerry wanted an office on the top floor of headquarters."

"And you?" asked Scully.

"I was gunning for an office in the basement with no heat or windows," said Mulder.

"I know what happened to you," said Scully. "But what about Jerry?"

"Jerry had some bad luck in Atlanta," Mulder said. "He was working on a series of hate crimes."

"What kind of bad luck?" Scully asked.

"Seems he misplaced a piece of evidence, bagged and everything," Mulder said. "By the time he found it, a federal judge had lost both hands and his right eye. It was a bit of a setback for Jerry."

"I can see where it might be," Scully said.

By now they had crossed the gleaming marble lobby and reached the bank of elevators. Mulder pushed an Up button. There was a loud *ping*, and the stainless steel door opened with a *whoosh*.

The inside of the elevator was stainless steel as well. Scully ran her eyes down a vertical row of

GHOST IN THE MACHINE

buttons on a control panel. She pressed 30. The door closed with another *whoosh*.

"Going up," a computer-generated voice announced, and the elevator moved smoothly upward.

"First floor . . . second floor . . . third floor," the voice announced.

Suddenly, without warning, the elevator jolted to a stop.

The sudden stop threw Scully to the floor.

After helping his partner to her feet, Mulder looked around the elevator. From a corner of the ceiling a scanner, its red light glowing, was looking down at them.

Scully spotted a door on the control panel marked EMERGENCY. She opened it and saw a phone.

Scully had hardly gotten the phone to her ear when a computerized voice said, "Hello. I am here to help you. Please give me your name."

"This is Agent Dana Scully," she said. "FBI."

"Please state the reason for your call," the voice said.

The elevator started moving smoothly upward once again.

"Please state the reason for your call," the voice repeated.

"Well," said Scully, "everything seems all right now. Thanks anyway."

15

THE X-FILES

She hung up, and exchanged puzzled looks with Mulder.

When the elevator door opened on the thirtieth floor, Jerry was waiting for them.

"Find anything?" Mulder asked as they headed toward Benjamin Drake's office.

"Sure did," said Jerry, beaming. He led Mulder and Scully to an opened panel on the office wall.

Inside was an electric circuit board.

"See here?" said Jerry. "Someone tampered with this switch. Changed the positive charge to a negative. Guaranteed to produce a high-power shock. And see this?"

He showed them a line from the circuit board that ran to the bathroom keyhole.

"When Drake stuck the key in—*finito*," Jerry said, pointing to the key still in the lock.

"Nice work, Agent Lamana," said Scully.

"Didn't know you were a such a techie, Jerry," Mulder said.

"Actually, some guy from the building filled me in on a few minor details," Jerry said. "Name of Peterson. Some kind of maintenance man."

"The key in the lock is safe to touch now?" said Scully. "I'd like to take a look at it."

"No way you can get it out of there," Jerry said. "It's fused with the lock." He shook his head. "Takes

16

GHOST IN THE MACHINE

a lot of juice to melt a steel key."

"And to throw a hundred-and-eighty-pound man ten feet," said Scully. She looked at the outline of a body marked on the tile floor. Above the sink was a wall mirror cobwebbed by cracks.

Meanwhile, Mulder had returned to the circuit board.

"The switch—was it moved by a human hand?" he asked.

Jerry scratched his head. "Well, we didn't find any prints."

"But *could* it have been?" Mulder asked.

"Uhhh . . ." said Jerry, hunting for something to say.

A voice from the doorway saved him the trouble.

"Sure it could have been switched manually," said a voice behind them. It was a voice of authority.

17

Chapter FOUR

The man in the doorway was solidly built. His pale beige suit contrasted with his dark skin. He looked as cool and competent as his voice.

Jerry introduced him. "This is Claude Peterson, the systems engineer for the building. He discovered the body."

"You say that someone could have set the electronic booby trap by hand?" Mulder asked Peterson.

"It's theoretically possible," Peterson said. "But first you'd have to override COS."

"COS?" asked Mulder.

"The Central Operating System that runs the building," Peterson answered.

"This COS, it runs everything in this place?" asked Scully.

"The whole shebang—and then some," said Peterson. "It controls everything from the lights to the elevators to the water in the toilets. It was Wilczek's brainchild."

"Wilczek?" Mulder asked.

"Brad Wilczek," Peterson explained. "He created COS. He insisted it be installed when this building

GHOST IN THE MACHINE

went up, no matter what it cost. He saw it as a pilot project for systems that would run every building from bungalows to the World Trade Center."

"I take it this Wilczek is the guiding light of Eurisko," said Scully.

"*Was* the guiding light," Peterson said, shaking his head. "Eurisko and he went their separate ways after the last stockholders' meeting."

Mulder and Scully exchanged a quick look. Then Mulder turned back to Peterson. "As systems engineer, I presume you would be capable of overriding COS?" he asked.

"Me?" Peterson responded, and shook his head. "Don't let my job title fool you. I'm just a glorified building super. All I do is monitor the system, make sure it's functioning okay. Like when I spotted the overload in this office and came in to check it out, and found . . ." He stopped there, grimacing at the memory.

"I take it that overriding COS demands a high degree of expertise," Mulder said.

"For openers, you'd have to break the access code, which is . . ." Peterson paused to calculate. "Let's just say it wouldn't be easy."

"We're going to need a list of everyone with that kind of know-how," Mulder said. "Can you make us one?"

THE X-FILES

"Sure," said Peterson. "But I tell you now, it's going to be a pretty short list."

"One more thing," said Mulder. "Does COS control the phone lines?"

"Sure, of course," Peterson said. "Wilczek was aiming for a total system."

"Does it monitor incoming calls as well as outgoing calls?" asked Mulder.

"Yes, it does," Peterson said. "Why?"

"Just asking," Mulder said.

"Can I go now?" Peterson asked. "Got to check on the ventilation on the tenth floor. I gave the agent here my statement, plus the number for my beeper at work and phone at home."

"If we need you, we'll ring you," Jerry said, nodding his permission to go.

As soon as Peterson had left, Jerry said to Mulder, "Why'd you ask about the phone?"

"Because the one in the bathroom is off the hook," said Mulder.

Jerry took a look in the bathroom and said, "Well, well. Yeah. It is. Matter of fact, I was just getting ready to check for stuff like this when you two came in."

"Perhaps Drake was talking to someone just before he did his Ben Franklin imitation," Mulder said.

GHOST IN THE MACHINE

Jerry gave him a blank look.

"You know, Ben Franklin and his kite," Mulder explained. "The key tied on the end of the string. The lightning flash."

"Sure. Of course. Got you," Jerry said. He gave Scully a big smile and slapped Mulder on the shoulder. "Taught him everything he knows."

"Everything you know, huh, Mulder?" Scully teased as Jerry walked out of the office.

Chapter FIVE

The next afternoon Scully found Mulder in his office feverishly hunting through the papers on his desk.

He had a lot of digging to do. Books, pamphlets, magazines, folders, and assorted objects covered the desktop.

"Lose something?" Scully asked.

"The notes I wrote on the Eurisko investigation," Mulder said distractedly, not looking up from his search.

"Maybe if you cleaned your desk more than once a year," said Scully. "Or is it once a decade?"

"I'm telling you, those notes were right here," Mulder insisted.

"No time to look for them now," Scully said. "It's after three. We're late."

"Point taken," Mulder said. He followed Scully out of his office and down the corridor.

In the conference room, a dozen other agents were already seated around a long table. At its head sat Special Agent Spiller. Scully smiled at her old instructor as she and Mulder hurriedly grabbed vacant chairs.

Spiller returned the smile with her usual expression, which was none.

"Glad to see you two managed to join us," she said curtly. "You're just in time to hear Agent Lamana's report."

Jerry Lamana didn't look at either Mulder or Scully. He kept his eyes glued to the yellow legal pad in front of him.

"'Both the statistical rarity of homicidal electrocution and the complexity of the crime itself indicate a very unusual kind of killer,'" Jerry read. "'After all, there are much simpler ways of murdering somebody.'"

Scully glanced over at Mulder. He shook his head in disbelief as he listened to Jerry's profile. Light began to dawn in Scully's eyes as she realized what was going on.

"All of which leads me to believe that our guy is some kind of antisocial game player," Jerry said. He was sounding smoother and more confident with every word.

Meanwhile, Mulder had managed to compose himself. His mouth, though, was a bit tight, as if he had swallowed a bitter pill.

"Maybe the killer is a recluse," Jerry continued, "since he designed a trap not only to avoid detection, but to avoid contact with the victim."

Scully could hold back no longer. She leaned

THE X-FILES

toward Mulder and whispered in his ear, "Mulder, is that your profile?"

Mulder turned toward her and mouthed the words *"Forget it."*

Meanwhile, Jerry had stuck a cassette into a player on the table.

"The phone call Drake received just before his death supports this theory," Jerry declared, and hit the Play button.

"At the tone, Eastern Standard Time will be seven thirty-five P.M.," a computerized voice stated.

"Drake's estimated time of death," Jerry said, turning off the machine.

Spiller leaned forward, interest sparking in her eyes. "Why would Drake call for the correct time just before he died?" she asked.

"It was an incoming call—from somewhere within the Eurisko Building itself," Jerry said. He paused for drama. When he was sure everyone was listening hard, he said, "The killer wanted to be sure Drake took the bait. A brilliant scheme, I must admit."

"And a brilliant analysis," said Spiller. There was the slightest hint of warmth in her voice. "Excellent work, Agent Lamana."

Jerry did his best to look modest. "Just trying to do my job," he said.

GHOST IN THE MACHINE

After the meeting, though, Jerry had a much harder task at hand. He had to face Mulder.

"What the devil are you doing?" Mulder demanded, cornering Jerry at a water cooler.

"Hey, old partner, don't get all bent out of shape," Jerry said.

"Those were *my* notes," Mulder said.

"I didn't think you'd mind," Jerry replied soothingly. "I mean, it's all in the family."

Mulder opened his mouth to respond, but he could think of nothing to say. Meanwhile, Jerry glanced around nervously to make sure no one was listening. Then he turned back to Mulder and declared, "Anyway, they were just rough notes. If you listened closely, you know I filled in all the blanks."

"Jerry, you went into my office and deliberately stole my work," Mulder went on, still trying to come to terms with it.

"Look," said Jerry, patting Mulder on the arm, "you're only on the case because I asked you to help me out. So that's what you did. You helped me out. What's the big deal?"

With that, he walked away.

Mulder looked after him, shaking his head.

"What'd Jerry say?" Scully asked, coming up behind Mulder.

THE X-FILES

Mulder turned and shrugged. "He apologized—in his own special way."

"Oh?" Scully responded, raising her eyebrows.

Mulder chose to change the subject. "Anything new on the case?" he asked.

"I just got off the phone with Peterson, the systems engineer," Scully said. "He gave me the list of people with the COS access code."

Scully handed Mulder a piece of paper.

He glanced at it and said, "One name? Brad Wilczek?"

"He said it'd be a short list," Scully said. "I've been doing some research in the financial press. It's headline news how much Wilczek hated Drake."

"Wilczek killing Drake makes sense," said Mulder. "That's the trouble. It makes too much sense. Only a crazy egomaniac would try anything so totally obvious."

"Which would indicate that Jerry's excellent psychological profile of the killer was right on the money," said Scully dryly. "You really should congratulate him."

"I'll do that," Mulder said. "Just as soon as we finish checking out Mr. Wilczek."

Chapter SIX

"Nice place to live," Scully said, looking out the car window. She and Mulder were driving past the green trees and rolling fields of the Virginia countryside.

"They used to call this horse country," Mulder said. "They probably still do. I believe the local bluebloods still ride to hounds and hunt foxes."

"I have a hunch that isn't Brad Wilczek's kind of thing," said Scully, as she turned the car down the long driveway to his home.

"I have a hunch your hunch is right," Mulder said, gazing at the gleaming, ultramodern structure at the end of the driveway. "That's not exactly your average old plantation house."

Scully parked behind a car already in the driveway, and they got out.

"Nice, again," she said, looking at the sleek vehicle. "A Fifty-seven Corvette. In mint condition. Must have *cost* a mint at auction."

Mulder looked at the license plate: EURISKO 1. He patted the gleaming hood, then looked at the house again. "So this is what an IQ of 220 and an

THE X-FILES

an annual salary in the millions can buy you."

"All this and heaven, too," Scully said.

"High-tech heaven," said Mulder, glancing at the security camera pointing down at them from above the front doorway. It swiveled to follow their every move.

"I don't think we have to ring the bell to say we're here," Scully commented as she pressed the button.

Her finger had barely left it when the door opened.

Brad Wilczek stood in the doorway. He looked like the photos Scully had seen of him in the newspaper clippings. Slight, wiry, and scruffy. But the photos hadn't captured the intense energy that radiated from him.

"Yes?" Wilczek demanded, the word coming out fast and clear as a spark in the dark.

"Brad Wilczek?" Scully asked.

"Yes," he said.

Scully flashed her ID. "We're from the FBI."

"What took you guys so long?" Wilczek said with a mixture of impatience and contempt.

Scully exchanged a look with Mulder. Wilczek might be many things, but humble was clearly not one of them.

"Come in," Wilczek said, already turning away

to lead them through the house. "Oh, and do you mind taking off your shoes?"

It was only then that Scully noticed Wilczek was barefoot.

Wilczek led them padding over marble floors, past indoor Japanese gardens under glass skylights and into a space dominated by a giant stainless steel desk. An impressive computer sat enthroned on top of it.

Wilczek perched on the edge of the desk. He motioned for Scully and Mulder to sit in a pair of chairs.

"What can I do for you?" Wilczek asked. Then, before Scully or Mulder could say a word, he answered his own question. "I assume you would like to know about my relationship with the late Benjamin Drake."

"If there's something you'd like to tell us," Scully said.

"You can divide the computer science industry into two types of people," Wilczek said. "Neat and scruffy. Actually, I suppose you can divide the world that way."

"I take it that you think Drake was one of the first kind," Scully said. As she spoke, she could not help glancing at Mulder. She caught him nodding to himself, a gleam of understanding in his eyes.

THE X-FILES

As she'd suspected, he and Wilczek were on the same wavelength.

"Neat people like things neat," Wilczek went on, a sharp edge to his voice. "They wear neatly pressed suits. They like to work with things you can add up or subtract neatly. Things like market shares and third-quarter company profits and personal bonuses."

"And you had a different vision for the company," Scully said.

"I started Eurisko out of my parents' garage," Wilczek said. There was pride in his voice. Pride, and a touch of sadness for a vanished past. "I was twenty-two years old. I had just spent a year following the Grateful Dead. My mind was wide open and I could feel the whole universe pouring in."

Scully found the picture Wilczek painted easy to imagine. His hair might be thinning a bit on top; there might be a few lines on his face. But the twenty-two-year-old kid with a dream seemed very much alive in every word he spoke, every gesture he made.

Wilczek paused, then asked, "Do you know what *eurisko* means?"

Mulder cleared his throat. "It's from Greek, isn't it?" he said. "It means *I learn things*."

Wilczek gave him a grudging, slightly surprised

30

GHOST IN THE MACHINE

look of approval. "That's close," he said. "But actually, it means *I discover things*."

With that, Wilczek hopped down from his desk. His voice turned bitter as he said, "Unfortunately, Ben Drake was not interested in discovery. He was a shortsighted, power-hungry, greedy human being with eyes only for looking out for Number One—and blind to everything else."

"Can you be more specific?" Scully said. "What exactly was Benjamin Drake blind to?"

"Blind to all the new possibilities of computer software application," Wilczek said, spitting out his words. "PDAs, artificial intelligence, the Smart Home."

"The Smart Home?" Scully asked.

Moving quickly, Wilczek led Scully and Mulder to an impressively large black cabinet. He opened it to reveal a large flat-screen monitor.

"This is the prototype of a system that someday will be used in every building built," he said. "With it, I have access to every square foot of my house."

Wilczek punched the Power switch.

A complex blueprint appeared on the screen.

"You see a detailed plan of the first floor of my house," Wilczek said. "Every door, window, stick of furniture, smoke detector, lightbulb, water pipe, electrical line, telecommunication gateway—the works.

THE X-FILES

Those charts indicate temperature and humidity. Those three red blipping lights show us standing here, and if there were any other moving object in the house, the system would track it, too."

"Impressive," Scully said, and Mulder nodded in agreement.

"Impressive? I'd say so," said Wilczek. "This place is as safe as Fort Knox and as energy efficient as your average igloo."

"When was the system installed?" Mulder asked.

"Three years ago," Wilczek said, his words underlined by anger. "Eurisko was that many years ahead of Microsoft and the other software biggies on the project. Then Ben Drake, in a typical stroke of genius, started choking off funds for it."

Mulder gave Wilczek a moment to cool down. Then he said, "Mr. Wilczek, is this system related to the one in Eurisko World Headquarters?"

"COS, you mean?" Wilczek said. "Sure. COS is a variation of the system here. The only difference is that it's bigger, which makes it even better. After I designed COS, I figured no one could deny that it was the wave of the future." Wilczek paused. "But Ben Drake proved me wrong."

Almost savagely, Wilczek punched off the monitor. He stared grimly at the dark screen.

"In your opinion, Mr. Wilczek," said Mulder,

"how many people know the system well enough to override it?"

"Ah, the bonus question," Wilczek said. There was a certain relish in his voice. "I was wondering how long it would take you to ask it. The answer is—not many."

"Could someone have hacked into the system?"

"Not your average phone freak," Wilczek said. "But there are plenty of kooks out there. Very talented kooks. Data travelers. Electro-wizards. Techno-anarchists. Even twenty-two-year-old kids working day and night in their garages. In cyberspace, anything is possible."

Scully stepped in. "Could you have done it?" she asked.

Wilczek answered with a smile. "Of course," he said. "I created the system. COS is my baby."

Then he said, still smiling, "But, of course, you might phrase it another way. You might say, COS could be my weapon. That's why you're here, isn't it? I'm the logical suspect."

"You don't seem too worried," said Scully.

"It's a puzzle, Ms. Scully," Wilczek said. "Scruffy types like me like puzzles. We enjoy walking down unknown avenues of thought. We delight in turning new corners. We like saying . . . *eurisko*."

Scully felt herself being drawn to this man. It

was hard for her not to feel sympathy for him.

Wilczek seemed to read her thoughts.

"One more thing about scruffy types," he said. "As a general rule, we don't commit murder."

Chapter SEVEN

"I'll do the field journal notes for today at home tonight," Scully told Mulder when they returned to his office. "It'll be safer there. You know, more secure."

"Jerry's not so bad," Mulder said, picking up on her meaning. "He's just . . . Jerry."

"Well, you know him better than I," Scully said. "And I'd just as soon keep it that way."

"Jerry does take some getting used to," Mulder agreed. "You might call him an acquired taste."

"Yeah, like hot fudge over tuna fish," Scully said with a smirk. "Of course, if you'd like to have him back as a partner, I'd be glad to step aside."

"I'll see you tomorrow," said Mulder. "I think I'll run some more checks on Brad Wilczek. As far as our suspect list goes, he seems to be the only game in town."

Back in her apartment that night, Scully found writing her notes both easy and hard.

It was easy to list the reasons to believe that Brad Wilczek was the man who had murdered Ben Drake.

First of all, Wilczek had the motive. He had

35

THE X-FILES

disliked Drake for a long time. And Drake's final termination of the COS project could have been the last straw.

Second, Wilczek had the skill. If anyone could have programmed the COS in the Eurisko Building to kill, Wilczek was the man.

Most important, Wilczek had the personality. The crime clearly was the work of a man who liked to play games. For a guy like him, the line between reality and virtual reality had to be close to invisible. He'd find it hard to see the difference between zapping someone on a screen or off it.

The trouble was, though it was easy to finger him, it would be hard to corner him. Wilczek, whatever else he was, was a genius. As Scully wrote in her last few sentences, "The problem is, there seems a strong possibility that Wilczek is a genuine genius, and would be a genius at covering his tracks. If Wilczek is so smart, how do we outsmart him?"

She read over her report, corrected a couple of typos, and clicked Save.

Tomorrow morning she'd put the report on a disk and take it to headquarters, safe from prying eyes.

She turned her computer off and went to bed, falling asleep quickly

She did not wake up when a low ringing sounded in the apartment. There was a series of beeps and

36

clicks as a modem connection was made. In the next room, the computer monitor lit up.

The report on Wilczek scrolled up the screen, from the first word to the last.

After a few moments the screen went dark again, as if it had never been on.

The next day in Mulder's office, Scully showed him her report.

He read it, nodding. It was exactly what he would have written.

Then he showed her what he had come up with. A set of digital audiotapes. Their labels read: BRAD WILCZEK, SMITHSONIAN LECTURE SERIES.

Then he handed her a tape marked PHONE MESSAGE RETRIEVAL, FROM EURISKO HEADQUARTERS COS.

"I believe we may find a comparison interesting," he said.

He was right. An hour later, Scully was still playing the tapes.

Wilczek's voice came out crystal clear: "From the beginning I knew that Eurisko would expand not by traditional Western ways of thought, but by employing certain Zen beliefs and other Eastern philosophies—"

Scully hit the Pause button. She did a quick rewind, then pushed Play again. "Eastern philosophies—"

T H E   X - F I L E S

Another pause, rewind, and playback:
"Eastern—"

Nodding, Scully hit Pause and extended her hand for Mulder to pass her another tape.

She was about to put it into the machine when she saw Mulder's eyes swivel toward the hall.

Jerry Lamana stood in the doorway.

"Give me a second," Mulder told Scully.

He stood up and went to Jerry. "What's up?" he asked. "As you can see, Agent Scully and I are quite occupied."

"I've got to talk to you," said Jerry.

Mulder glanced at Scully. "Why don't we go out in the hallway to discuss this?" he said.

Jerry did not move. "Look," he said, "I'm here with my hat in my hand. I fouled up. I'm sorry. What more can I say?"

"All you had to do was ask," Mulder said in a pained voice. "I would have helped you with your profile."

"You don't know what it's like, Mulder," Jerry said.

"What what's like?" asked Mulder.

"You heard about Atlanta," Jerry said.

Mulder nodded.

"That got me on six months' probation," Jerry said, his voice moving toward a whine. "I've gotta file daily reports like a new agent."

"It was bad luck," Mulder said. "Could have happened to anybody."

"Not to you," Jerry said in an accusing voice.

"Don't run yourself down, Jerry," Mulder said soothingly. "You're a good agent. We did some good work together."

Jerry shook his head. "Let's face it. I was just tagging along."

"That's not how it was," Mulder said—but his protest lacked force.

"How would you know, Mulder?" Jerry said. "You were too busy dazzling them up there on your high wire. Just like you're doing now. You're off doing your thing on this case. And I'm left in the dark."

"Not at all, Jerry," Mulder declared, not looking at Scully this time. "As a matter of fact, it's a good thing you showed up. Saved me a phone call. Agent Scully and I want your opinion on some material we're checking out. Right, Scully?"

Scully forced a smile. "Right. Come right in, Agent Lamana."

They sat in front of a large computer monitor. The computer was hooked up to two digital audiotape machines. It was, as Jerry had remarked, "quite a gadget."

"It produces computerized spectrograms," Scully informed him. "It was developed by the voice biometrics lab at Georgetown University."

"For what?" Jerry wanted to know.

"It has the capacity to identify individual speech patterns," Scully explained.

Jerry shook his head in wonder. "Yeah, like I said, it's quite a gadget."

He scratched his head as Scully said, "Look at this."

She hit Play on one of the tape machines.

A computerized voice said, "At the tone, Eastern Standard Time will be seven thirty-five P.M."

On the screen, the sound of the voice appeared as a spectrogram—lines and bars in a range of gray and black.

Scully saved the image.

She played the second tape. On it were words and syllables spliced from Wilczek's lecture series. They came out jumpy and uneven, but distinct.

"At the tone, Eastern Standard Time will be seven thirty-five P.M."

On the monitor screen, another spectrogram appeared.

"Now we'll stack the two," Scully said, and punched out the command.

The two spectrograms appeared on the screen, one above the other.

Scully punched out another command.

The computer highlighted the same words on the two spectrograms, moving from word to word and syllable to syllable.

"You were right, Mulder," Scully announced, freezing the screen.

"Right about what?" Jerry asked.

Scully didn't bother answering. Instead she picked up a wax pencil.

"Look at the first syllable of the word *Standard*," she said. The syllable had been left highlighted on both spectrograms. Scully's wax pencil circled them triumphantly. "It's identical on both graphs. Both come from a single voice."

Light dawned on Jerry's face. "Then you're saying that the voice from the lecture and the voice on the phone call were the same," he said. He sounded enormously pleased at his insight.

"I'm saying that both voices are Brad Wilczek's," Mulder said. "He electronically disguised his own voice. But he couldn't alter underlying rhythms and intonations unique to his own speech patterns."

"Which means he's the one who killed Drake," Scully said. "He had the motive. He had the means. And now we have the evidence."

She pulled her jacket from the back of her chair and started to put it on.

"I'll buzz over to Judge Benson in Virginia," she

THE X-FILES

said. "I can get an arrest warrant for Wilczek in less than an hour."

Jerry stood up, too. He already had his jacket on. "Somebody has to make sure Wilczek stays put. A guy like that, you never know what he'll do."

Mulder was thinking the same thing.

"I'll go with you, Jerry," he suggested.

"*No,*" said Jerry, his tone turning fierce.

"But perhaps it might be best . . ." Mulder said gently.

"Let me bring him in alone," Jerry said, pleading now. "I need this one, Mulder."

Without waiting for a reply, Jerry was out the door.

Chapter EIGHT

Brad Wilczek was having trouble.

Not with Ben Drake's death. As far as Wilczek was concerned, the world was better off without Drake. Certainly Eurisko was. Drake had promised to free Eurisko from money worries by selling shares of it to the public. Instead the company had fallen into the hands of people who cared nothing about what Eurisko could do for the world, only what it could do for their bank accounts.

Not with those snoops from the FBI, either. Wilczek could run rings around them in cyberspace. Besides, he even found the guy, what was his name, Mulder, okay. There was a look in his eyes, an intensity about him that Wilczek could dig. As for the other one, Scanlan, Solly, Scully, she seemed simply out to get the facts and would follow wherever they led. That was cool with Wilczek. He had always believed in letting discoveries take him as far as they could.

What Wilczek was having trouble with was the one thing he'd thought he could trust.

COS.

THE X-FILES

It was like being betrayed by his best friend. Or more exactly, his own child. That's what COS was, his brainchild, and no father could have loved his child more.

But now he was trying to log on to the system, and it was like pounding on a locked door.

He sat in front of his computer and read the message that kept appearing on the screen.

"ACCESS DENIED."

"Rats," Wilczek muttered. He felt like punching out the screen, shattering the plastic with his fist.

Instead he punched out another command.

It let loose a series of random passwords at high speed. They scrolled down the screen like lightning. But the answer was always the same.

"ACCESS DENIED."

"Come on, open up," he muttered. The keyboard clicked like a machine gun as he typed out an elaborate command.

Finally he hit Enter.

"ACCESS DENIED," the system answered once again.

Wilczek's shoulders slumped as he shut his computer down. Shaking his head, he stared at the darkened screen.

Then he stood up and walked through his huge house to the front door. There he put on a pair of

GHOST IN THE MACHINE

tattered running shoes and went out.

He reached his Corvette, got in, and roared off, making up for lost time.

He raced down the road, not bothering to look in his rearview mirror.

If he had, he would have seen a car moving off the side of the road to follow him.

A half hour later, Wilczek screeched to a stop in front of the Eurisko Building. The parking area was almost empty. The working day was over. He got out of his car and ran into the building, not looking back.

If he had, he would have seen the trailing car stop behind the Corvette and Special Agent Jerry Lamana jump out.

Wilczek did not pause as he ran by the seated security guard.

"Mr. Wilczek," the guard called out easily, as Wilczek tore by.

The guard had been with Eurisko for ten years. He knew Wilczek well enough not to blink at anything he did. After all, Wilczek was a genius, and geniuses did their own thing.

The guard, though, did stop the plump guy who came pounding into the building next. Even when the man flashed his FBI badge, the guard looked at him suspiciously.

THE X-FILES

Jerry Lamana demanded, "Where did Wilczek go?"

"You might try the top floor," the guard said finally. "That's Wilczek's office. At least it used to be."

Jerry didn't pause to say thanks. He ran to the elevator bank. He pressed a button, and the door whooshed open. He got in and pressed the top-floor button, and the elevator smoothly started up. Jerry kept his eyes fixed on the indicator as the floor numbers flashed by. He did not look up at where the red light of a computer scanner glowed. He did not see the camera swiveling to zero in on him as he stood trapped in the elevator.

Chapter NINE

Brad Wilczek held his breath as he inserted his card key into his office door. His ex-office, anyway.

He pushed, and the door swung open.

He smiled thinly. Ben Drake hadn't had a chance to change the lock.

He snapped on the light and headed straight for the computer on the desk.

He sat down at his old desk. It felt like coming home.

He might have used some of the millions of dollars he had made at Eurisko to build his dream house, but this desk was where his dreams had been born. This was where he belonged.

He ran his fingers lightly over the computer keys.

He could shut his eyes and remember how it had felt in the beginning, when he was so young and the future was everywhere he looked. That was before the door to the future swung closed in his face, slowly at first, then with a bang.

At least they hadn't shut COS down, he thought. It was still working. And he still had the power to make it work for him.

THE X-FILES

He hoped so, anyway.

He sat up straight in his chair and started typing in a command.

He paused, clicked Enter, and held his breath.

"Welcome back, Brad," the computer said.

Wilczek's mouth dropped open.

Stunned, he sat motionless for a moment.

Then he began clicking the keys again. As he typed, he spoke the words he entered:

"You are not equipped with a voice synthesizer. When was this modification made?"

The machine made no reply.

Wilczek's fingers flew again.

"What is my user level?"

Wilczek heard the computer whirring. Beneath that sound, he could hear his own heartbeat.

"That is now a decision to be made by the Operating System," the computer voice told him.

"Let's see if I can influence that decision," muttered Wilczek.

His forehead furrowed in concentration, he tapped out the series of commands that should give him control over the system he had designed.

"Sorry, those commands are not available at your current user level. Try again," the computer voice told him.

Try again. But try *what*?

Maybe no one had changed the lock on his

GHOST IN THE MACHINE

office door. But somebody had changed the lock on the COS command center. His brain spun and his fingers flew as he searched for the right keys to open it.

Suddenly he froze. Flashing onto the monitor was the image of a man's face.

The face was plump and flushed. The eyes stared upward intently.

Wilczek could hear a computer-generated voice announce, "Twenty-sixth floor."

"What the—" Wilczek said, and quickly typed, "What are you doing?"

The computer said nothing, and the picture on the monitor changed. Now the whole man could be seen, in his dark polyester suit, with his sweat-damp button-down white shirt and limp tie. He was standing in the stainless steel elevator.

"Twenty-seventh floor," the computer announced.

The man in the elevator smiled in eager anticipation. He patted a bulge in his suit near his armpit.

"Shoulder holster," Wilczek said to himself. "Must be more FBI."

"Twenty-eighth floor," said the computer.

"What are you doing?" Wilczek typed frantically.

"Twenty-ninth floor," the computer said. "Thirtieth fl—twenty-ninth—thirt—twen—"

Wilczek jumped up from the desk. He ran to a

49

THE X-FILES

row of monitors on the office wall. All of them showed the same picture of the man in the elevator.

Wilczek pulled open the control panel under the monitors. Frantically he flipped switches. Nothing he did had the slightest effect.

"Thir—twe—thir—" the computer spat out like a machine gun.

Now the sensor was picking up the voice of the man in the elevator.

"What the—" the man said, as the elevator jolted to a stop, and the doors whooshed open.

The man stared through the open door at the concrete wall of the elevator shaft.

"What are you doing?" Wilczek shouted at COS.

Meanwhile, the man in the elevator was pressing the Emergency button. He punched it harder and harder, again and again.

Sweat was pouring down his face when he finally gave up. He stood there in silence.

A creaking came from somewhere. Then a tapping noise. Then silence again.

"Going down," the computer announced.

The man's mouth opened wide. He lost his footing as the bottom of the elevator dropped out from under him.

He was thrown against the wall, his head smashing against the stainless steel as the elevator plummeted.

GHOST IN THE MACHINE

Through the open door the concrete shaft went by in a blur as the man lay sprawled on the floor.

"No!" Wilczek screamed.

His scream died in his throat as the scene on the screen jumped, then flickered like a candle.

The last thing he saw was the man's legs twitching, then becoming motionless, before the picture went black.

"Program executed," the computer said.

Chapter TEN

Scully felt rotten. She had an unpleasant taste in her mouth.

She hadn't exactly been supportive of Jerry Lamana during the investigation. And now he was dead.

She reached Mulder's office door, swallowed hard, and knocked.

There was no answer.

Funny, she thought. It might be late at night, but she had been sure she'd find Mulder here. He had been burning the midnight oil from the start of the Eurisko case. Now he had to be working harder than ever.

Scully tried the door. It was unlocked, as usual, she noted wryly. She opened it, entered, and saw Mulder sitting in the dark in front of a video monitor. In his hand was a remote control. He was clicking the button rapidly, slowing the action, freezing it, speeding it up, then going to playback to check it out again.

Scully watched him for a couple of minutes. He didn't notice she had entered. His eyes were glued to the monitor.

Finally Scully cleared her throat and said, "I've been looking for you. I had a hunch I'd find you here."

Mulder didn't answer. He was still engrossed in the video.

Scully tried again. "I heard about Jerry."

That made Mulder look up.

"I'm really sorry," she said gently.

Mulder nodded softly.

There was a long moment of silence.

Then Mulder said, "I don't think Wilczek did it."

"What?" Scully asked, startled. She had never before seen Mulder's judgment unbalanced by emotion. But there was always a first time.

"It doesn't make sense," Mulder said firmly. "Why would he have come back to Eurisko?"

Scully shrugged. "Maybe he wanted to destroy evidence," she said. "Maybe he wanted to make sure he had covered his tracks."

"If you were going to destroy evidence, would you pose for the cameras?" Mulder said. "Look at this video. It shows Wilczek in his old office. He had to know a camera was recording his every move. He was the one who installed it there."

"Maybe it slipped his mind," Scully suggested.

"Maybe if Wilczek had an ordinary mind—but not the one he has," Mulder said. "Here, watch the the video." He pressed Rewind, waited a moment,

THE X-FILES

then pressed Play. "Does this look like a man committing murder?"

Scully watched Wilczek enter the office. She watched him work furiously at the computer. She watched him leap up to go to the row of monitors and wrestle with the control panel below them. Finally she watched Wilczek running like a madman out of the office right after the monitors went black.

"Who knows what goes on in a mind like that?" said Scully. "Maybe he went back to his old office to gloat. Maybe he wanted to play with his favorite toy one last time. Or maybe it was as simple as a compulsion to return to the scene of the crime. And maybe when he saw Jerry coming up after him, he panicked and lashed out like a cornered rat. I'd say that that last possibility is very strong."

"I tell you, I believe that something is wrong with that picture," Mulder insisted. "Very wrong."

Scully bit her lower lip. It was painful to see Mulder like this, deaf to reason.

"Listen to me, Mulder," she said. "You've been through a lot—more than I think you even realize."

Mulder, stone-faced, shook his head.

He turned away from Scully to rerun the video again.

"Mulder—" Scully began.

GHOST IN THE MACHINE

"I tell you, Wilczek's smarter than this," Mulder said as he watched Wilczek silently screaming at COS.

Scully sighed.

"Mulder," she said, "Brad Wilczek just signed a confession. How much more proof do you need?"

There was a sharp click from the video remote control.

The monitor went dark.

But Mulder kept staring at it.

"Mulder—" Scully began, and stopped when she saw that he was paying no attention to her. His eyes were frozen on the black screen.

"Scully—" he said finally.

"Yes?" she said.

"I think I'd like to be alone for a while," he said. "I have some thinking to do."

"Right," she said. She turned and left the office, shutting the door softly behind her.

She automatically opened her mouth to remind Mulder to lock it—but stopped herself in time.

Jerry Lamana wasn't there to kick around anymore.

She had to forget him—just as Mulder had to.

They had to put the whole case behind them.

She knew she could. But could Mulder?

Chapter ELEVEN

Mulder turned his car onto Brad Wilczek's driveway.

Chances were he'd be able to get by Wilczek's home security system. Without Wilczek there to monitor it, any alarm would be like a tree falling in the middle of the forest.

Mulder rounded a bend in the driveway and saw a car in front of Wilczek's house.

It wasn't Wilczek's vintage Corvette. Not even close. It was a run-of-the-mill sedan that you'd never notice on the highway. Unless you were Mulder. He recognized the car the moment he saw it. Just the way he recognized the three men standing near it. He did not know their names, but he knew what their hard faces and the bulges in their suit jackets meant.

They were very polite, as Mulder knew they would be. They would stop being polite only when absolutely necessary. It was not wise to make it necessary.

When Mulder got out of his car and started toward the house, one of the men smoothly stepped in front of him.

GHOST IN THE MACHINE

"Excuse me, sir," the man said. "This is a crime scene. You'll have to leave."

"Yeah, I know," Mulder said. "I have a search warrant."

He pulled it from his pocket.

The man did not bother to look at it. His two partners came up to flank him. Neither of them looked at the warrant, either. They all looked at Mulder with eyes as cold and flat as mirrors.

"Look, I'm with the FBI," Mulder said. He flashed his ID.

None of the men blinked.

"This warrant is no longer in effect," the first one said.

"What are you talking about?" Mulder responded. "I just got it this morning. The judge's signature is barely dry."

As he spoke, Mulder tried to look past the men to see what might be going on in Wilczek's house.

That only made the men step closer, blocking Mulder's view and forcing him a step back.

"Unless you have Code Five clearance, I'll have to ask you to turn back," the first man said.

"Code Five clearance?" asked Mulder. "But the only ones who have that are—"

"The only ones who have entry into this house at the moment," the first man cut in.

THE X-FILES

Mulder looked from one man to another. It was like looking at identical bricks in a solid wall.

Still, they had told him what he needed to know.

He knew that there was only one thing he could do in order to find out anything more.

There was someone he had to get in touch with. That someone was a man of many secrets—secrets that included his name and his role in a government agency as secretive as he. He called himself Deep Throat.

He was not an easy man to get in touch with. But Mulder knew that there were ways. Ways that even those with Code Five clearance didn't know.

"Thanks for coming," Mulder told Deep Throat.

It was lunchtime in the big plaza in front of the Eurisko Building. The space was lit by bright sunshine and jammed with office workers enjoying the fresh air. Deep Throat had chosen the time and place for this meeting. It was calculated to help him fade into the crowd, just as his gray three-piece suit was. Even his gray hair and pale skin seemed part of his design. Deep Throat was a master of the art of invisibility.

Mulder himself was wearing sunglasses, as a

kind of gesture of respect for Deep Throat's passion for staying out of sight.

Still, Deep Throat was annoyed, as Mulder knew he would be.

Deep Throat did not like to surface. He liked to contact Mulder, not the other way around. He liked to make it clear who was in control at all times. Control was something he refused to lose.

"I'm here against my better judgment," he told Mulder as they strolled across the crowded plaza. His gaze darted everywhere to make sure no one paid them the slightest attention. No one did. "In the future, I insist that you respect the terms of our agreement."

"Sorry," Mulder said. "But there's information I can only get from you. Important information. I need to know why Brad Wilczek is the subject of a Code Five investigation. That usually involves only the most sensitive areas of military security. What interest does the Department of Defense have in him?"

Deep Throat had to smile. Mulder's questions were often a source of amusement—since Mulder frequently knew the answers. It was like a game whose goal was to make Deep Throat give the official stamp of truth to suspicions from outside the loop. Fortunately for Mulder, Deep Throat loved games.

"Why do you think they'd be interested in the boldest and most brilliant computer programmer in the world?" Deep Throat asked. He paused at a hot dog stand and held up one finger to signal his order.

Mulder did the same. As both men put mustard on their hot dogs, Mulder asked, "The people in Defense want Wilczek to create software?"

Deep Throat took a bite, swallowed, and said, "Over the years, Mr. Wilczek has thumbed his nose at the most tempting offers to develop advanced guidance for weapons systems." Deep Throat's mouth curled in contempt as he used a paper napkin to wipe mustard off his upper lip. "Seems Wilczek doesn't approve of war. He's a true bleeding heart."

"What kind of software?" Mulder asked, as they started strolling again.

"How much do you know about artificial intelligence?" Deep Throat asked.

"I thought it was only a far-out theory," Mulder said. "Something for science fiction writers only. Not a possibility that anyone actually took seriously."

"No one did—until two years ago," Deep Throat said. "Do you remember that chess match in Helsinki, Finland? When the computer beat a grand master? It was the first time a machine ever

GHOST IN THE MACHINE

produced a better chain of reasoning than the finest human mind."

"I read about it," Mulder acknowledged.

"Did you think about it—and what it might mean?" Deep Throat asked.

"I thought about it," Mulder said.

"Then you'll be interested to know that that champion chess-playing computer was programmed by Brad Wilczek," Deep Throat said. He looked up at the bright sky, where white clouds drifted. One of them crossed the sun, and a chill shadow swept over the plaza. "Rumor was, Wilczek did it by developing the first adaptive network."

"An adaptive network?" asked Mulder, to make sure it meant what he thought it did. It was something too major to risk getting wrong.

"A learning machine," Deep Throat confirmed. "A computer that absorbs experience and is altered by it. A computer that continually improves its functioning. In other words, a computer that actually thinks."

"Artificial intelligence," said Mulder, blinking behind his shades as the sun came out again. "So it *is* possible."

"Possible enough to make some people in the Defense Department ache to get their hands on it," Deep Throat said.

61

THE X-FILES

"I can see that," said Mulder. "I can see where they might be willing to do almost anything."

"The question is," Deep Throat said, looking hard at Mulder, "what can *you* do?"

Chapter TWELVE

After meeting with Deep Throat, Mulder was more convinced than ever that he was right about Brad Wilczek. That Wilczek had confessed to the murders in order to protect COS.

He had to go see Wilczek and convince the computer genius that what he was doing was wrong. Dead wrong.

Fortunately, Mulder's FBI badge was enough to get him into the cell where Wilczek was being held. The men from the government might have been able to put Wilczek's house out of bounds. But the Federal Detention Center in Washington, D.C., was still Mulder's turf.

Wilczek's cell had blank walls on three sides and bars from floor to ceiling on the fourth. There was no TV, no books, no newspapers. Wilczek had been left alone to stare at the windowless walls or through the bars and think things over.

Wilczek was sitting in a chair, counting specks on the ceiling, when Mulder came in. Wilczek's face had two days' stubble of dark beard. There were circles under his eyes. And his T-shirt and jeans had been replaced by a dark blue prison uniform.

There was one other difference as well.

"As you see, they make me wear shoes all the time," he told Mulder.

"Good to see you looking so well," Mulder said, making meaningless conversation.

As he spoke, he swiftly moved around the cell, running his eyes over every nook and cranny.

Wilczek smiled.

"You can save yourself the trouble, Agent Mulder," he said. "I've already checked for bugs. Both the living kind and the electronic variety. There are none. You can believe it. I've had lots of free time to look. Besides, it stands to reason—why would they want to bug me? I've already given them what they want. They have my signed confession. Which brings me to the question: What do you want, Agent Mulder? Or did you simply come here to gloat?"

"I want a simple piece of information," Mulder said.

"What is it?" asked Wilczek. "My shoe size?"

"Tell me why you're willing to spend the rest of your life in prison for a crime you didn't commit," Mulder said.

"What are you talking about?" Wilczek asked. "I'm guilty. You must have read my confession. And

64

GHOST IN THE MACHINE

I assure you, as I will assure the court, that I signed it of my own free will."

"I know you're innocent," Mulder said. His voice was matter-of-fact, as if he were adding up two and two.

Mulder's eyes met Wilczek's. Their gazes locked. There was a long moment of silence. Then Wilczek looked away. But he said nothing.

"You're protecting a machine," Mulder said in the same level voice. "You're protecting your brainchild, the Central Operating System at Eurisko."

There was another pause.

Finally Wilczek said, "If I'm protecting anything—it's not the machine."

"Then what *are* you protecting?" Mulder demanded, his voice suddenly intense, like a light switch turned on.

Again there was a pause.

When Wilczek spoke, his voice sounded distant. It was as if his words were coming from deep within him.

"I once read the life story of Robert Oppenheimer," he said. "You know of him, I presume."

"The American scientist who led the team that developed the atomic bomb," Mulder said.

Wilczek nodded and went on. "After they dropped the bomb on Hiroshima and Nagasaki in Japan,

Oppenheimer spent the rest of his life regretting he had ever glimpsed an atom."

"Oppenheimer may have regretted his actions," Mulder said, "but he never denied that he was responsible for them. He was who he was, he did what he did, and he did not try to hide or escape from it."

"Oppenheimer was a scientist who loved his work," Wilczek said, his voice now full of feeling. "His mistake was in putting his work in the wrong hands. The hands of those whose job was to kill." There was pain in Wilczek's voice. The pain that Oppenheimer must have felt. And his own.

"People make mistakes," Mulder said.

"I won't make that mistake," Wilczek declared.

"But your machine killed Drake," Mulder said. "And it killed my friend."

Wilczek looked away, avoiding Mulder's accusing eyes. After a moment, he stiffly said, "I'm sorry about what happened—but there's nothing I can do."

It was Mulder's turn to speak with feeling now. "You talk about the evil of killing. You're afraid of the government finding out what COS can do and getting their hands on it. But you're willing to take a chance COS will kill again."

Wilczek shrugged weakly. "It's the lesser of two evils," he muttered.

GHOST IN THE MACHINE

"What about a third choice?" Mulder demanded.

Wilczek said nothing. But the look he gave Mulder was questioning.

"You created that cursed machine," Mulder said. "You can figure out a way for me to destroy it."

Chapter THIRTEEN

"Mulder, I'm worried about you," Scully told him.

"Don't be," Mulder said. "We have more important things to worry about."

Mulder had called her and set up a meeting at the Eurisko Building plaza in the late afternoon. It was best to be out of doors when they talked, he said. They had reached a stage in the investigation where the highest security was necessary.

That made Scully worry even more. It was not a good sign when a person started imagining that people were spying on him. It indicated a certain . . . strain.

Now as they walked side by side, Scully said, "I don't follow you, Mulder. What stage of the investigation are you talking about? The investigation is over. It's history. Wilczek has confessed. He's not even attempting an insanity plea. The only question left is how many years in the slammer he'll get."

Mulder shook his head. "His confession is a lie. He's taking the fall for COS. He doesn't want cer-

GHOST IN THE MACHINE

tain people to know its capabilities. He wants to keep them from trying to get their hands on it."

"Look, Mulder, I know you don't want to believe Wilczek is guilty," Scully said. "But facts are facts. No computer system could kill on its own."

"COS could," Mulder said.

"You've been listening to Wilczek too long," Scully said. "He's clouded your judgment with his high-tech pep talk. He's been making a pitch for computers his whole life. But it's clear that he's blaming the machine as a last resort. A desperate one. And a bad one."

"It's the only thing that makes sense," Mulder insisted. "The COS project was losing big money for Eurisko. Drake was about to kill it. COS has eyes and ears throughout the Eurisko Building. It learned of Drake's plan. And it was the one that did the killing."

"Come on, Mulder," Scully said, shaking her head. "You're trying to tell me that the machine murdered Drake in self-defense?"

"In self-preservation," Mulder said. "It is the first law of life. It is the primary instinct of all living creatures."

"But COS isn't alive," Scully said. "It can't feel. It can't think."

"But what if it can?" Mulder asked.

THE X-FILES

"Mulder, that level of artificial intelligence is decades away from being achieved," Scully said.

"Then why has the government been trying to tap in to Wilczek's research?" Mulder demanded. "What do they know that you don't want to believe?"

"Who have you been talking to?" Scully asked.

"Sorry, you'll have to trust me on it," Mulder said.

"Are you sure you're not just hearing voices?" asked Scully, looking at Mulder with fresh concern.

Mulder ignored her doubt. "The important thing is, Wilczek can develop a virus to destroy COS," he said.

Scully stopped walking, making Mulder stop as well. "Mulder, I don't know quite how to say this."

"Say what?" Mulder asked.

"I think you're looking for something that isn't there," Scully said gently. "I think the death of Jerry Lamana has affected you more than you realize. I think you want to find a cause for that death as big as the guilt you feel about it. I think it might be a good idea if you went to talk to someone—someone who could help."

Mulder looked at Scully.

After a moment, he spoke. "You're probably right," he said. "See you tomorrow."

He turned to move away.

"Where are you going?" Scully asked.

"To talk to someone," Mulder said, and walked quickly off across the empty plaza into the sunset.

It was the middle of the night, and Brad Wilczek was lying in the dark with his eyes open.

He couldn't sleep, and even if he could have, he didn't want to.

It was like the old days, he thought, when he was working on an idea, feeling his brain going all out, full blast. The excitement was the same.

The energy. It was what he had lived for his whole life long.

But now there was a difference. A big difference.

In the old days, his excitement came from creating something new.

Now destruction was on his mind.

Suddenly the light flashed on in his cell.

He heard the click of a lock and the cell door being opened.

Mulder stood in the doorway, the guard behind him.

"Could you please leave us by ourselves?" Mulder asked the guard. "I have to go over some confidential material with the prisoner. Highly classified."

"Sure you'll be safe?" the guard asked. "The prisoner may be . . . emotionally stressed. Possibly violent."

"That's all right," Mulder assured him. He patted his pocket. "I can handle it."

"Yes, sir," the guard said.

The guard closed the door and went back down the hall.

"You've decided?" Mulder asked, as soon as he was sure the guard was out of listening range.

"Yes," Wilczek said.

"You'll do it?" Mulder asked.

"Yes," Wilczek said.

"*Can* you do it?" Mulder asked.

"I think so," Wilczek said. "Maybe. I'll have to see. Or rather, you'll have to see. The thing is, COS has undergone certain changes. Changes I may not be aware of. Changes it made on its own."

Mulder laid a slender laptop computer on Wilczek's bed. He had carried it under his trench coat.

"How long will you need?" Mulder asked.

"Come back in a couple of hours," Wilczek said, flipping up the laptop screen. He turned the computer on. His fingers hovered over the keyboard as it warmed up. "I think I can give you what you want. Then it'll be your turn."

Chapter FOURTEEN

Scully did not enjoy writing her field notes that night. When she was finished, she turned her computer off and went to bed.

She tossed and turned in her sleep, buffeted by bad dreams.

It was almost a relief when her ringing phone woke her up.

Scully decided to let her answering machine take the call. The phone rang once more, then stopped. But instead of the familiar sound of her voice on the outgoing message, Scully heard a series of high-pitched tones. Tones she recognized as the sound of a modem making a connection over the phone line.

Wide awake now, Scully jumped out of bed and headed toward the computer in the living room. But she wasn't quick enough. Through the doorway of the bedroom she saw the computer monitor light up.

Scully ran to it. She saw a sequence of commands flashing, starting with "WILCZEK.DOC."

She stood frozen as her field report scrolled up

THE X-FILES

the screen. When it reached its end, there was another series of beeps, and the computer shut down.

Scully did not hesitate. She grabbed the phone, punched out a number, and told the operator at the other end, "This is FBI Special Agent Dana Scully, ID number 2317-616. I need a quick trace on a modem connection made just now to phone number 202-555-6431."

The answer came in minutes. As soon as Scully heard it, she said, "Thank you," slammed down the phone, and started throwing on the first clothes she could find.

"Rats," Mulder said to himself.

He was parked near the Eurisko Building. He had just gotten out of his car and was moving to open the trunk when he saw headlights approaching on what had been a deserted street.

The arriving car skidded to a stop behind his.

Scully jumped out. Mulder raised his eyebrows. For once in her life, Scully was not a model of neatness. It looked as if she had dressed in the dark.

"Mulder!" she called, her voice anxious.

"What are you doing here?" he asked.

"Someone—or something—has been scanning my computer files," she said. "Probably tapping my

GHOST IN THE MACHINE

phone as well. It accessed information about this case from my computer files. I traced the line to the source of the data theft . . ."

Scully paused and gazed up at the Eurisko Building, looming high and dark above them.

"It came from somewhere in there."

"It's the machine, Scully," Mulder said.

Scully did not argue. She merely said, "How do we get in?"

Mulder smiled and opened his trunk.

"Remember the Trojan horse?" he asked, and took a license plate and a screwdriver out of the trunk.

Scully looked at the license plate.

It read EURISKO 1.

"You had access to Wilczek's car?"

"It's wonderful what an FBI badge can do," Mulder commented, and began replacing the license plate of his car with Wilczek's.

That job finished, he got behind the wheel with Scully beside him. He drove to the steel door of the parking garage under the Eurisko Building.

"Rank has its privileges," said Mulder. "Let's see what Wilczek's can do."

An overhead light from the doorway scanned the license plate.

There was a click of recognition, and the massive door slowly lifted.

75

THE X-FILES

"Open sesame," Mulder said, and moved the car slowly through the opening.

The car was halfway in when a steel arm swung down, blocking the car's path.

"What the—" said Mulder.

"Mulder!" gasped Scully as she looked up through the side window and saw the steel door dropping like a guillotine.

A moment later, she was staring through shattered glass.

Behind her, the car roof had caved in. A passenger in the backseat would have had a flattened head.

Her whole body was shaking, and her ears were deafened by the car alarm going off full blast.

"I think our car trip is over," said Mulder as he struggled to get the door on his side open. Finally he succeeded and climbed out. He reached back into the car to grab a black knapsack, then helped Scully get out of the car.

"So much for the element of surprise," he said, shouting over the blaring alarm. He lifted the engine hood and pulled a wire. The sudden silence seemed almost as loud as the ear-splitting din.

His voice seemed to echo in the empty garage as he said, "I don't think taking the elevator in this building is a good idea. What say we try the stairs?"

"Sure," Scully said. "It'll be good for me. Been skipping the health club too much lately."

The stairwell was lit by high-wattage lights. But on the twenty-fifth floor, as Mulder and Scully paused to catch their breath, the lights went out.

"Mulder?" Scully said in the blackness.

"Trick or treat," he replied, and a beam from a flashlight he took out of his knapsack lit the stairs going up.

When the flashlight shone on the number 30, they stopped climbing and made their way to the door that led out to the executive offices.

A green light was flashing near the door handle.

"Looks like it's open," Scully said.

She reached out toward the handle—but Mulder grabbed her wrist.

"Hey, ouch," she said. "What's the idea?"

"Take the flashlight," Mulder said, handing it to her.

Mulder took a thick rubber glove and a screwdriver from his knapsack.

"Let's not make the same mistake Benjamin Drake did," Mulder said, slipping the glove on.

With his gloved hand he inserted the screwdriver tip into the door lock.

There was a sizzling flash as Mulder dropped the screwdriver and jumped back.

"Owe you one, Mulder," Scully said.

But Mulder wasn't listening to her. He was listening to the door bolt sliding shut.

"May I have the flashlight?" he said, extending his hand.

Scully handed it to him, and Mulder played its beam along the edge of the door.

"Too narrow to slide a piece of plastic through," he said. He examined the lock. "Takes a card key. No way to pick it."

Then he shone the flashlight upward, to where a scanner looked down on them, its red light glowing.

"Somehow I think we're not alone," he said. "We haven't been since we got in here."

"Every inch of this building must be watched," Scully said, and paused. "Watched by . . . *it*."

Mulder glanced up at the glowing red light.

"What are you looking at?" he growled, and pulled off his rubber glove.

Standing on tiptoe, he shoved the glove over the camera lens.

"Now, while we still have a little privacy, let's see if we can find a weak spot in the security system," he said.

Slowly he played the flashlight beam around the walls.

He and Scully saw the grill in the ceiling above the door at the same time.

GHOST IN THE MACHINE

"It's part of a ventilation system," Scully said. "Which means it opens into an air duct."

"There might be a way to go through the duct to the other side of the door," Mulder said.

"I'll go," Scully said. "I'm smaller than you. A better fit."

Mulder couldn't argue. "Well, if the duct fits . . ." he said, handing Scully the flashlight and screwdriver.

Mulder linked his hands palms upward to make a stirrup. Scully used it to boost herself up, the flashlight and screwdriver tucked under her belt.

"I can just make it," she said.

She reached up, unscrewed the grill, and let it drop to the corridor floor.

She craned her neck and shone the flashlight into the opening.

"No telling where the duct goes," she said. "But it is big enough for me to crawl through. Wish me luck."

She tucked the flashlight and screwdriver back under her belt. Using both hands, she hoisted herself up and over the edge of the opening.

Chapter FIFTEEN

The air duct Scully was crawling through was stainless steel. The metal reflected her flashlight beam blindingly. Scully was going in what she hoped was the direction of the executive office. There had to be another ventilation grill there. She'd unscrew it, drop into the office, and let Mulder in from the stairwell.

Except that she couldn't seem to find it.

Her calculations must have been off, she thought. Or perhaps she had lost her sense of direction and followed the wrong branch of the system. She decided to keep going the way she was headed a bit longer. If she stayed lost, she'd have to—

She did not get a chance to decide what she'd do.

She could no longer go the way she had been going.

A howling wind hit her in the face, stopping her like a stone wall.

She felt herself being pushed back by that wall of wind, into a branch of the duct she had passed previously.

GHOST IN THE MACHINE

It took her a moment to understand that the wind was not pushing her.

As bits of paper and other debris whistled past her head and brushed and bounced off her face, she realized she was being pulled backward. Something was sucking the air into the duct.

Scully grabbed hold of a protruding edge of a section welding. Desperately hanging on to it with one hand and holding her flashlight in the other, she managed to turn herself around to face the source of the suction.

Her flashlight showed a gigantic fan whirling at the end of the duct. Its blades were a murderous blur.

The force of the fan was overwhelming. As it continued to pull the air in, Scully's fingers were torn from their hold. She bounced down the duct, helplessly clawing at the smooth steel. She saw the blades coming closer and closer, growing larger and larger.

There was a pipe running down the inside of the duct, and she grabbed it with one hand as she went past it. She held on to it and tried to brace her feet against the curving side of the duct.

Here goes nothing, she thought as she heaved the screwdriver, then the flashlight, at the fan, hoping to jam it.

THE X-FILES

The fan chewed them up like a dog crunching dry food.

"Come on, Scully, at least go down fighting," she told herself, and drew her FBI-issue .45 automatic.

Gritting her teeth, squinting down the barrel, she started emptying her bullet clip at an impossible target.

"Scully?" Mulder said as he heard the door bolt click open and saw the green light come on.

She made it, he thought, relief flooding through him. He shouldn't have worried. He should have known she could do it.

Then the door opened, and his stomach seemed to drop into his shoes.

It wasn't Scully in the open doorway.

It was Peterson, the Eurisko Building systems engineer.

"Agent Mulder," Peterson said, his eyebrows rising. "What are you doing here?"

Before Mulder could answer, a distant sound froze him.

It might have been thunder, except that the night outside was dry and clear, stars shining bright.

Or it might have been gunshots.

Peterson, though, had another explanation.

"COS has been acting up lately," he said. "That

GHOST IN THE MACHINE

elevator crash that killed your sidekick was just the beginning. Since then all kinds of weird stuff has been going down. And tonight things are really snafued. Strange sounds are just part of it. There have been power surges. Lights going on and off. That's why I'm here so late. Trying to get a handle on it. Got to admit, though, it's too much for me. Like I said before, I'm just a glorified maintenance man."

"Can I take a look at it?" Mulder asked.

Peterson shrugged and led the way to the executive office computer.

He stepped aside to let Mulder past. Quickly Mulder ran his fingers around the sides and back of the machine.

"Where's the B port?" he wondered aloud.

"Some things I do know," Peterson said, and opened a panel in the side. A column of ports was revealed.

Before he let Mulder start working, though, he asked, his forehead furrowed, "You sure you know what you're doing? Because if you don't, it's my job on the line."

"Wilczek's instructions were quite precise," Mulder assured him.

From his knapsack, Mulder took a black box the size of a large cigarette lighter and plugged it into the B port.

83

THE X-FILES

The computer came to life, lights blinking.

"My oh my," said Peterson, scratching his head in wonder.

"Rats," said Mulder as he read the message on the monitor.

"ACCESS DENIED."

His mouth a thin line, Mulder took out another small black box and plugged it into the C port.

He punched out a series of numbers on the keyboard and waited.

Asterisks filled the screen like shooting stars.

Then a voice announced, "System access granted. User Code Level Seven."

Peterson's mouth dropped open.

Mulder's mouth curved in joyful triumph.

He reached into his knapsack and pulled out the virus diskette Wilczek had made for him. He remembered Wilczek's eyes, bleak and bleary with sorrow, when he handed over the diskette.

Mulder was poised to shove the disk into the drive when Peterson's icy voice stopped him cold.

"Not bad, Agent Mulder," Peterson said.

Mulder turned his head. He stared into the barrel of a large gun.

"Thank you, Agent Mulder," Peterson said. "I've been trying to access Level Seven for the past two years. Now please stand back."

Chapter SIXTEEN

Mulder stared at Peterson's gleaming gun. Then at the cast-iron expression on his face. He put two and two together. It added up to his being an idiot for not putting things together sooner.

"Defense Department?" he said.

Peterson shrugged, holding his gun steady. "Close enough," he said. "Let's just say our paychecks are signed by the same person."

Mulder winced as questions pricked at his mind. Why hadn't Deep Throat clued him in to Peterson's real job? Was there a level of secret government beyond even Deep Throat's depth? Or had Deep Throat simply been testing Mulder?

If so, Mulder had failed the test. Peterson waved his gun at Mulder and said, "Step away from the machine and hand over the diskette."

When Mulder hesitated, Peterson leveled his gun at Mulder's chest and said, "Don't test my determination, Agent Mulder. I have full authorization to do whatever I have to do."

Mulder tensed—and so did Peterson's trigger finger.

85

For a moment, time seemed to stand still.

"Put down the gun," said a voice behind them.

Scully stood in the doorway. Her clothes were in tatters, her face smudged with grease and grime, her hair a total mess. But the gun in her hand did not tremble as it pointed dead at Peterson.

Peterson still held his gun on Mulder as he turned his head toward Scully. "You may think you know what you're dealing with, but let me tell you that—"

"Shut up and drop the gun," Scully said, her voice rising.

Peterson heard her anger. He let his gun drop onto the carpeted floor.

Shaking his head, he warned, "You're making a mistake, Agent Scully. A big mistake. You're violating your sworn duty."

Mulder's stomach lurched as he saw a shadow of doubt in Scully's eyes.

Peterson saw it, too. He went on, his voice stronger now, "This operation is more important than you can possibly imagine. It has been authorized by people in the very highest places. It has the greatest value for the security of our country. It—"

Mulder's voice cut him off. *"Don't listen to him, Scully!"*

Scully's eyes moved from one man to the other as if watching a tennis match.

GHOST IN THE MACHINE

Peterson said, "The technology in this machine can make America number one in—"

"The machine is a monster, Scully," Mulder interjected. "It's already killed two people. The government won't be able to control it any better than Wilczek could."

Peterson's voice turned threatening. "Make no mistake, Agent Scully. You will be held responsible if you interfere with this operation. Not only your job will be in jeopardy. Your freedom will be. And perhaps your very—"

"Scully, think of those who already have died, and those who will in the future," Mulder urged.

Scully looked at Peterson. She looked at Mulder.

Mulder could see what Scully was going through.

He had put her on the spot. She was torn between her loyalty to the bureau and her loyalty to him. Between doing her job by the book and letting him rewrite the rules.

It wasn't the first time he had put her on that spot. He had put her on that spot ever since they had teamed up.

He knew what her choice had been all the times before. But he didn't know what it would be now.

Scully looked from him to Peterson and back again.

"Put in the disk, Mulder," she said.

"Right, Scully," Mulder said.

"You're wrong—you don't know how wrong you are," Peterson said ominously.

But no one was listening to him.

Mulder took a deep breath, shoved the disk into the slot, and held his breath as he waited.

He did not have to wait long.

It took a few seconds for the machine to ask in a hurt voice, "What are you doing, Brad?"

Then the question turned to pleading. "Brad, don't do this."

Numbers, letters, and symbols scrolled down the screen at incredible speed. Millions of them. Billions, perhaps. Mulder could not begin to calculate how many. He could only blink as they went by.

Lights on the computer console flashed on and off in a crazy pattern.

The lights in the office went on and off. From outside came the sounds of doors swinging open and slamming shut, elevators screeching as they ran full speed up and down their shafts until their cables snapped.

From those ear-splitting sounds came a picture of the whole huge building thrashing and groaning like a wounded animal. An animal going into spasms of agony as one electronic arrow after another ripped into it.

From the computer in the office a cracking voice

GHOST IN THE MACHINE

babbled, "Security Zone Seven . . . Five . . . Going up . . . Going down . . . Hello . . . Goodbye . . . Hello . . . Goodbye . . . Hel . . . Goo . . . He . . . G . . ."

Mulder leaned closer to the machine to catch the last words of its fading voice:

"Why, Brad?"

Chapter SEVENTEEN

The voice ended. The lights went out. There were only silence and darkness.

Then, room by room, floor by floor, the lights in the Eurisko Building came on again.

It was as if the whole building had awakened from a sleep.

Or rather, a nightmare.

Mulder wiped sweat from his forehead. Scully wiped a patch of grease from hers. Peterson shook his head, his face grim.

"It had to be done," Mulder told him. "Sorry, Peterson—if that's your name."

"It'll do as well as any other," Peterson said in a tight voice.

"I realize you were doing your job," Mulder said. "You felt you were doing the right thing. But Agent Scully and I felt the same way. It was a conflict between different points of view. Those things happen."

Mulder and Scully left Peterson looking at the burned-out computer monitor. He did not say a word as they headed out of the office. He just stood there, staring at the blank screen and shaking his head.

Mulder's first question when he arrived at the detention center was, "What do you mean Brad Wilczek is no longer here? Has he been released?"

"I am sorry, but that is privileged information," the official said without missing a beat.

"I am an agent of the Federal Bureau of Investigation I'm assigned to this case," Mulder insisted.

"I'm sorry, but you do not have the necessary clearance," the official answered in the same automatic, almost bored voice.

Five days later, the storm of fury within Mulder was still rising. But his shoulders were slumping. By that time, he had exhausted all normal sources of information. He had punched up every data bank file he could think of. He had approached every high-ranking person in every branch of the government that he knew. And he was still at square one.

He had only one last source to try to tap.

Deep Throat, however, gave Mulder a bit of a surprise. He was far more sympathetic than Mulder had expected when they met in the Eurisko Building plaza.

Winners, of course, could afford to be sympathetic. And it was the look of a winner that Deep Throat gave Mulder.

"I've checked with Congressman Klebanow and the Department of Corrections subcommittee about Wilczek's whereabouts," Mulder told him. "I even petitioned the Attorney General's office."

"You won't find Wilczek," Deep Throat assured him.

"You can't just take a man like Brad Wilczek without explanation," Mulder insisted.

"*They* can do whatever they want," Deep Throat said flatly.

"But where is he?" Mulder wanted to know.

"He is in the midst of serious discussions with government officials," said Deep Throat. "Officials who have the power to grant him important favors in return for his help in certain areas. It is what we in the business call hard bargaining."

"Brad Wilczek will never make a deal," Mulder said fervently. "He'll never agree to work for them. He has his own vision of the future—and it's not theirs."

"Let me remind you that Wilczek's future for as far as the eye can see is in a small cell without access to even the most primitive computer," Deep Throat said, still smiling. "Lack of freedom does

GHOST IN THE MACHINE

strange things to a man. Remember, Wilczek's already confessed to two murders."

"He can have those confessions thrown out," said Mulder.

"That might depend on the judge selected to try the case," said Deep Throat. "And remember, the only evidence that could positively clear him is no longer there. The machine is . . . kaput. You made sure of that."

Mulder bit his lip. "But what else could I have done?" he asked.

"Nothing," Deep Throat told him. "Not unless you were willing to let the machine survive."

"So the Defense Department didn't find anything left," Mulder said.

"You may console yourself with that at least," Deep Throat said. "They've been at it for five days. Wilczek's virus did a thorough job. It left no trace of artificial intelligence. Even as we speak, the agents are winding up their search in there." Deep Throat gestured toward the Eurisko Building. It was ringed by police barriers and armed guards.

"Nothing, then?" Mulder asked.

"The machine is dead."

Chapter EIGHTEEN

When Claude Peterson was growing up, his father gave him a motto to live by:

"Winners never quit, and quitters never win."

Those words spurred him through high school and college. They pushed him step by step up the ranks in the government agency he worked for. They got him to where he was now, arguing with his boss over the phone.

"Sir," he said, "I sincerely believe it would be wise to continue our investigation for a few more days at least. The computer system is very complex. I feel that there still remains some possibility that—"

The voice on the other end of the phone cut him off. "Peterson, you have a team of twenty men, all experts in the field, right?"

"Yes, sir," Peterson said.

"You have been working in the building for five days, right?" the voice continued. The voice was not computer-generated. It merely sounded that way.

"Yes, sir," Peterson said. "Five days *and* nights."

"You have found absolutely no trace of any remaining artificial intelligence, right?" the voice said.

"No, sir—I mean, yes, sir," Peterson said.

"Do you have any idea of the expense involved in an investigation like this—and the difficulty we sometimes have justifying our budget?" the voice asked.

"Yes, sir—I mean, not exactly, sir," Peterson said. "That is not my area of expertise."

"I regret to say that it *is* mine," the voice said. "Our agency has more profitable areas in which to spend our money. Therefore, you will terminate your investigation. Have it cleaned up and closed down within five hours."

"But, sir—" Peterson began.

"That means by 1700 hours, you and your people will be out of there," the voice said. "Do you understand?"

"Yes, sir," said Peterson wearily.

"Any questions?" the voice asked.

"No, sir," said Peterson.

"Then *do it*," the voice said.

Peterson heard the click on the other end and hung up the phone.

Around him in the executive office, technicians were going through what was left of the Eurisko Building Central Operating System with microscopes, stethoscopes, electronic sensors—everything but fine-toothed combs.

More words from Peterson's childhood scrolled across his mind:

> *Humpty Dumpty sat on a wall,*
> *Humpty Dumpty had a great fall.*
> *All the King's horses*
> *And all the King's men*
> *Couldn't put Humpty*
> *Together again.*

Peterson sighed, then said in a loud voice, "Listen up, people. We have five hours to finish up here."

He was answered by groans and grumbling. He had a good team. They were no happier to give up than he was.

He made his voice stronger: "Those are orders from the top."

A man near him muttered, "Yeah. Ours is not to reason why. Our is but to stop doing and let die."

"Aw, come on, Sam," the man working next to him said. "This machine *is* dead, face it. You win some, you lose some."

Peterson made a note of the second man's name. He wouldn't be on any team Peterson headed again.

Nevertheless, Peterson had to say, "Come on, let's start clearing out of here."

He gave a quick glance around to make sure his people had begun packing up. Then he left the room. He didn't feel like sticking around to watch the end.

He wasn't there to peer under a pile of computer parts and see three lights flash on one after another. If he had, he would have sworn they were winking at each other.

He didn't see the red light on the scanner blink on, checking out the scene to see how close the crew was to leaving.

He wasn't able to speculate that nothing was beyond the powers of pure intelligence—not even the ability of COS to put itself together from scratch.

And he couldn't guess what its plans for the future might be.

THE TRUTH IS OUT THERE
for Young Adult Readers

Don't miss the new X-Files series
coming soon from

Voyager

An Imprint of HarperCollinsPublishers

Book One

The Calusari
by Garth Nix

Based on the characters created by
Chris Carter

ISBN 0 00 648324 0

Chapter One

The train whistled as it rounded the corner, the half-size red locomotive steaming powerfully, the brass fittings gleaming. All the children aboard were laughing and waving, happy to be at Lincoln Park.

A dark-haired boy stood by the fence that bordered the railroad track, watching the miniature train go past without any sign of enjoyment. A pink helium balloon bobbed above his head, held there by a silver string clutched in the boy's hand.

"Charlie!"

Someone called his name, and he turned to look. His mother, Maggie Holvey, beckoned him over. His younger brother, Teddy, was next to her, his bright blond hair shining. He was laughing, a happy child, so different from Charlie with his sullen expression. Teddy held another balloon by a silver string, and his mother held him by a leash attached to the harness securely buckled around his little two-year-old body.

"Come on, Charlie," called Maggie, her voice colored with the Romanian accent that had not disappeared after nearly ten years in America. Until she spoke, she seemed like any other American mom.

Charlie, watching Teddy, didn't respond. Suddenly Teddy smiled and waddled away from Maggie, reaching out to someone approaching through the passing crowd of parents and children. Their father, Steve Holvey, was coming over, carefully balancing two ice-cream cones in each hand.

"Charlie . . . Hey! Ice cream!" Steve called out. But even ice cream didn't seem to interest Charlie. Face devoid of any emotion, the balloon bobbing along above his head, he walked over to join his father, mother, and brother.

Unlike Charlie, Teddy really did want the ice cream, and reached for it too soon. Walking was still something fairly new for him, and the combination of balloon and ice cream too difficult. With a wail he fell forward, smearing ice cream over a face suddenly crumpled, smile gone in an instant. His balloon slipped through his fingers, streaking up into the sky, to be taken off northward by the wind.

"Shush, Teddy. Don't cry," soothed Maggie, picking up her younger son. "We'll get you another balloon, honey."

Promises don't mean much to a two-year-old. Teddy kept on bawling, tears mixing with the chocolate ice cream on his face. Without thinking, Steve grabbed Charlie's balloon and handed it to Teddy.

"Look. Here's your balloon."

Magically Teddy stopped in mid-bawl, once the string was safe in his pudgy hand and the pink balloon was floating above him. Charlie watched, a flicker of some emotion passing across his face for the first time.

"Such a mess!" exclaimed Maggie, looking down at her small, chocolate-stained son. "We have to get you cleaned up. Steven . . ."

"Yeah, sure . . . go on. Charlie and I will wait for you," replied Steve, sighing with relief that catastrophe had been so easily averted. Realizing he was still holding three ice creams, he offered one to Charlie.

"Eat your ice cream before it melts."

Charlie didn't move, hands still at his sides, ignoring the cone held out to him.

"I want my balloon."

"Yeah. Okay. We'll get you another one . . ."

"No," said Charlie vehemently. "I want *my* balloon."

"Fine, we'll get you another balloon!" exclaimed Steve, but Charlie still wouldn't take the ice cream. Finally Steve shrugged and tossed all three cones into a nearby trash can, muttering about the waste of money. If it wasn't one kid spoiling their day out, it was the other . . .

The park bathrooms were very basic. All stainless steel and concrete, the sinks were bolted to the wall and held up by steel posts. Maggie finished wiping off Teddy's face, then tied his halter leash to the sink stand and checked the knot to make sure it couldn't come undone.

"Okay, Teddy. I'll be right out." She smiled down at him before entering a stall and closing the door.

As it clicked shut, Teddy let go of the balloon, happily watching it float to the ceiling and bounce there, unable to escape into the open air.

There was a gap under the stall door, and Maggie

bent down to look through it as she sat, reassured by the sight of Teddy's little legs all wrapped up in bulky blue trousers. She started to sing, to reassure him that she was close by.

"There were six in the bed and the little one said, 'Roll over . . . roll over . . .'"

But Teddy wasn't listening to her singing. He was watching the balloon. It had suddenly begun to move, as if pulled down by an invisible force. Lower and lower it came; then it moved out—toward the outside door. As it reached the door frame, the toilet flushed.

Maggie kept singing as she tucked her shirt back into her jeans.

"There were five in the bed and the little one said, 'Roll over . . . roll over . . .'"

She ducked down again to see Teddy's legs for a second, and kept singing as she unlocked the door.

"They all rolled over and one fell . . ."

She opened the door and the singing stopped, her mouth open, no sound coming out. Teddy's halter was hanging from the sink. Empty. There was no sign of her precious child.

Or the balloon.

Panicked, Maggie dashed for the door, already shouting.

"Teddy! Teddy!"

Teddy wasn't far away, but he didn't hear her. All his concentration was on the balloon that floated just ahead of him, always out of reach. He was stumbling along as fast he could go, little arms reaching out. But always as his fingers closed, the silver string jumped away and the balloon led him farther on—down the lawn, and through the whitewashed gate that was open just enough for him to slide through. Finally the balloon stopped and Teddy smiled, reaching up for it . . .

Only Charlie saw the little boy cross the fence. His dark eyes were wide open, piercing the crowd, his father standing unaware beside him. But Charlie didn't say anything, didn't suddenly shout. He didn't do anything you'd expect from a boy seeing his little brother lost and wandering . . . wandering into danger.

Back on the lawn a man bent over his camera, looking through the viewfinder at his wife and children posing with one of the park's people-size animals. This one was a pink pig, even pinker than the cotton candy his children were smearing all over themselves. Satisfied with the shot, he clicked the shutter and looked up, his eye suddenly focusing on a very small child and a pink balloon in the background.

For a second he didn't think about where the child was; then the whistle of the miniature train—suddenly closer than it had been—made him realize.

"There's a kid on the tracks!" he shouted.

Steve was only a few yards away when he heard the shout, back at the balloon stand with Charlie. He wheeled around to look, a terrible stab of fear hitting him in the gut as he saw the blue suit and the pink balloon. It was Teddy, standing on the train tracks—and the train was already rounding the last corner, steaming at full speed toward his boy.

"Oh my God!" he groaned, already starting to run, a shout then exploding out of him: "Stop the train!"

Maggie, looking through the crowd at knee level, heard his shout and instinctively knew that Teddy was in danger. She started running toward her husband's voice.

Steve ran, his mind refusing to acknowledge the fact that he couldn't make it in time. The train was too close and Teddy just wasn't moving. Desperately he shouted again, willing his son to move, just a few feet, just a few inches, off the track . . .

"Teddy! Get off the tracks!"

Charlie followed him at a walk, still watching his brother. Charlie seemed in no hurry, as if he knew he would arrive at just the right time to see whatever would be seen.

Inside the locomotive the driver smiled back at his passengers. He'd been picked to drive the train because he looked like an old-time engineer in his Casey Jones hat and he could smile nicely. That smile vanished in a flash as he looked ahead and saw the child standing on the tracks, oblivious to the train's approach. Instantly his hand shot out to pull the emergency brake, but it had no effect on the train. He tried the brake again, but there was nothing, and the kid still hadn't even looked. Reaching up, he pulled the whistle cord again and again, the shrill noise blaring out, drowning the calls of the adults as they ran toward the tracks. Surely the kid would hear . . .

Teddy hummed the "Roll over" song and pulled at the balloon, happy that he had it back again. He didn't hear the whistle, or the shouts.

He never knew when the train hit him, whistle still blowing as it ended his short life.

"No!" screamed Steve as the red blur of the train passed just in front of him and Teddy went under, the pink balloon caught for an instant before the sharp wheels cut the silver string and it snapped away.

Then the train was gone and Maggie was there, hands held to her mouth to try to stifle the scream that waited to burst forth. Behind her, other parents used their hands, too, shielding their children's eyes, turning them away from the awful scene on the railway tracks.

Only Maggie went forward, kneeling down to pick up her dead child, cradling him as if she might somehow bring him back to life with her love. Steve, face blank with shock, looked on, unable to move or speak.

Back in the crowd, Charlie watched too, his face as expressionless as it had been all day. His father hadn't had time to buy him another balloon, but there was one floating behind him now, trailing a shredded piece of string. Untethered, it hung in midair. Almost as if it were held there, waiting. . .

LES MARTIN has written dozens of books for young readers, including the RAIDERS OF THE LOST ARK and INDIANA JONES AND THE TEMPLE OF DOOM movie storybooks, and many Young Indiana Jones middle-grade novels. He has also adapted many classic works of fiction for young readers, including THE LAST OF THE MOHICANS, EDGAR ALLAN POE'S TALES OF TERROR, and THE VAMPIRE. Mr. Martin is a resident of New York City.